Where are the Pontipines?

Andrew Davenport

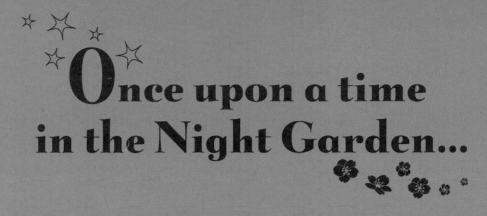

Once upon a time in the Night Garden...

The Pontipines came to play.

The Pontipines are friends of mine,
Although they're only small,
And even when there's ten of them,
They're hardly there at all.

One day, the teeny-tiny
Pontipines went for a
very long walk.

Through the log,

around the tree stump,

behind the flowerpots,

up a tree,

down again,

and in and out of the teeny tiny hole.

What a very long walk!

Over the bridge,

under the branch,

up and over Upsy Daisy's bed,

through the long grass.

What a very, very long walk.

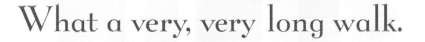

The little Pontipine children were feeling tired.

Wait a minute, Mr and Mrs Pontipine.
Where are the children?

Mi-mi-mi-mi-mi!

said Mr Pontipine.

Mi-mi-mi-mi-mi!

said Mrs Pontipine.

Mrs Pontipine looked through her binoculars.

Do you know what she saw?

Look at that.

The teeny tiny
Pontipine children
were feeling so tired,
they had all
gone to sleep in
Upsy Daisy's bed.

Only Upsy Daisy
is allowed to
go to sleep in
Upsy Daisy's bed!

Upsy Daisy!
Upsy Daisy!

Who's here?

It's Upsy Daisy!

Wake up little
Pontipine children!
Upsy Daisy is coming back.

But the teeny tiny Pontipine
children were fast asleep.

Boing!

Upsy Daisy sat down on her bed.

Boing...

The teeny tiny Pontipine children all woke up.

Boing... boing... boing... boing!

Upsy Daisy bounced
on her bed.

Boing... boing... boing... boing!

The teeny tiny
Pontipine children
bounced too.

And do you know
what happened?

The teeny tiny Pontipine children bounced right out of Upsy Daisy's bed!

Up, and up, and up they went.

Miiiiiiiiiiiiiiiiiiiiiiiiiiiiiii!

And down,
and down,
and down...

...into the little chimney of the teeny tiny Pontipine house.

The teeny tiny Pontipine children went

mi-mi-mi-mi-mi!

all the way home.

Isn't that a pip?

Once upon a time
in the Night Garden,

the teeny tiny
Pontipine children
went to sleep in
Upsy Daisy's bed.

Boing!

The teeny tiny Pontipine children bounced all the way home.

Thank you, Upsy Daisy.

Time to go to sleep everybody.

Go to sleep, Pontipines.

Go to sleep, Upsy Daisy.

Go to sleep, Makka Pakka.

Go to sleep, Tombliboos.

Go to sleep, Haahoos.

Go to sleep Ninky Nonk
and go to sleep, Pinky Ponk.

Wait a minute.
Somebody is not in bed!
Who's not in bed?
Igglepiggle is not in bed!

Don't worry, Igglepiggle...
it's time to go.